# Karen's Secret Valentine

Lauren.n
Rm 17

**Other books by
Ann M. Martin**

*Leo the Magnificat*
*Rachel Parker, Kindergarten Show-off*
*Eleven Kids, One Summer*
*Ma and Pa Dracula*
*Yours Turly, Shirley*
*Ten Kids, No Pets*
*Slam Book*
*Just a Summer Romance*
*Missing Since Monday*
*With You and Without You*
*Me and Katie (the Pest)*
*Stage Fright*
*Inside Out*
*Bummer Summer*

THE KIDS IN MS. COLMAN'S CLASS series
BABY-SITTERS LITTLE SISTER series
THE BABY-SITTERS CLUB mysteries
THE BABY-SITTERS CLUB series

# Little Sister

# Karen's Secret Valentine
## Ann M. Martin

### Illustrations by Susan Tang

A
**LITTLE APPLE**
PAPERBACK

SCHOLASTIC INC.
New York Toronto London Auckland Sydney

*The author gratefully acknowledges*
*Gabrielle Charbonnet*
*for her help*
*with this book.*

ISBN 0-590-69190-2

Copyright © 1997 by Ann M. Martin. All rights reserved. Published by Scholastic Inc. BABY-SITTER'S LITTLE SISTER is a registered trademark of Scholastic Inc. LITTLE APPLE PAPERBACKS is trademark of Scholastic Inc.

12 11 10 9 8 7 6 5 4 3 2 1          7 8 9/9 0 1 2/0

Printed in the U.S.A          40

First Scholastic printing, February 1997

# 1

# Nancy's Mittens

"Wait!" said Nancy. "Wait for me! I cannot find my mittens!"

I skidded to a stop. The recess bell had just rung. Everyone in Ms. Colman's second-grade class was rushing outside. I was almost out the door. I love recess!

"Did you look in your pockets?" asked Hannie, lifting one of her pink fuzzy earmuffs.

Nancy Dawes and Hannie Papadakis are my two best friends. I have two of lots of things. I will tell you why soon.

"What?" I cried. "Lost your mittens! You naughty kitten. Now you shall have no pie."

Nancy and Hannie laughed.

"I had them this morning," said Nancy. "I do not remember where I put them."

"You cannot go outside without mittens," I said. "It is freezing out there."

Our school, Stoneybrook Academy, is in Stoneybrook, Connecticut. It was Friday, the last day of January. There was about a foot of snow on the ground. And it was soooo cold.

"My mittens are on a string," I said. "I cannot lose them."

"My mommy bought me clips for mine," said Hannie. She showed Nancy how her mittens were clipped to her coat sleeves.

"Wait!" said Nancy. "Here they are, in my cubby." She grabbed her red mittens and put them on. "Now the Three Musketeers are ready to go outside."

"Yea!" I cried.

So now you know. The Three Musketeers are Nancy, Hannie, and me, Karen Brewer. We are all seven years old. (I am the youngest seven.) This is what we look like: Hannie has long dark hair in two ponytails. (Ponytails are when they are long and straight. Pigtails are when they are shorter and curlier. I decided that by myself.)

Hannie lives across the street and one house down from my daddy's house. I call Daddy's house the big house.

Nancy has red-brown hair and freckles. She lives next door to Mommy's house. Mommy's house is the little house.

I have blonde hair and blue eyes and more freckles than Nancy. And I wear glasses — a blue pair just for reading up close, and a pink pair for the rest of the time.

When the Three Musketeers pushed through the doors to the playground, I gasped. Going from a warm inside to the cold outside makes me feel tingly.

"We can't play hopscotch," said Nancy. "There is too much snow."

"I know," said Hannie. "Let's swing high on the swings and then jump off into the snow!"

"I do not know if Ms. Colman will let us," I said. Our teacher, Ms. Colman, was on recess duty that morning. She is gigundoly nice. But she will not let kids do things that are dangerous.

"Also," I said, "I am not sure if I am ready to jump out of a swing."

"Oh, okay." Hannie nodded. She knew what I meant.

Last month I had an accident. I had to have an operation. Now I am all better, but I am still a tiny bit afraid to do *some* things.

"Hmm, what can we do?" Nancy tapped her mitten against her cheek, thinking. "Tammy and Terri are on the seesaw."

Tammy and Terri Barkan are twins in our class.

"Addie and Audrey are playing ball," said Hannie. She pointed to Addie Sidney

4

and Audrey Green. They were taking turns bouncing a ball against the lunchroom wall. Addie's wheelchair had left tracks in the snow.

"I know!" I said. "Mommy says, when life hands you a lemon, make lemonade. So . . . when life hands you snow, make a snowball! We can have a snowfight."

Hannie grinned. "All right. Let's make a bunch of snowballs. We can throw them at the boys."

"Yes," I said. "But I will try not to hit Ricky." Ricky Torres is my pretend husband. I did not think it would be nice for a wife to throw snowballs at her husband.

Nancy stooped down and started patting snowballs into shape. "I am glad I found my mittens," she said. "They are perfect for making snowballs."

Soon we had a nice pile of snowballs.

"Let the snowfight begin!" I cried.

# My Best Enemy

*Pow!*

"Gotcha!" I crowed.

Bobby Gianelli dug snow out of his coat collar. Bobby used to be the class bully, but he is not so bad anymore.

"I'll get you for that, Karen Brewer!" he yelled, starting to make his own snowball. But he was smiling. Snowfights are fun.

I laughed, and ducked behind the monkey bars.

Hannie hit Ricky with a snowball.

Nancy hit Omar Harris on his leg.

Now all the boys began to scoop up snow.

We needed help. "Addie! Audrey!" I called. "Girls against boys. Come on!"

Addie wheeled herself over to our side. I dumped a pile of snow on her wheelchair tray. In about two seconds she had made three snowballs. She threw one and hit Hank Reubens in the chest.

"All right!" She punched the air.

*Wham!* Just then a snowball hit me right in the face. Snow covered my glasses. Snow went in my mouth. Snow stuck to my hat. It was cold and wet. I wiped my mittens across my glasses.

"I am sorry," called Hank. "I did not mean to hit you in the face. Are you okay?"

"Yes," I called back. I grinned. "But we are going to get you back!"

All of us girls scooped snow and made snowballs faster than ever. Well, almost all of us. My best enemy, Pamela Harding, was standing by the oak tree. Her two best friends, Jannie Gilbert and Leslie Morris, were standing with her. They probably did not want to get cold and wet. Well, for heaven's sake.

I leaned down and began to make an extra-large snowball. I packed on layers of snow, and patted them hard.

"Heh, heh," I chuckled. "I will get Hank with this."

I stood up.

"Watch out, Karen!" cried Hannie.

I was pelted by snowballs! I could not see a thing. I pulled my arm back and threw my snowball as hard as I could.

"Oh! Ow, ow, ow!" someone shrieked.

I brushed snow off my glasses. I looked around. Who had I hit? Not Bobby. Not Hank. Not Omar.

Guess who it was. Pamela. And I had gotten her right in the face. Her hat was on the ground. Her hair and face were covered with snow.

"Oops. I am sor — " I began.

"You dumbhead!" yelled Pamela.

I had not meant to hit Pamela. It was an accident.

"It is not nice to call names," I said.

"You and your stupid baby snowfight!" cried Pamela.

"Snowfights are not stupid," I said.

"Older kids have snowfights, too," said Nancy.

"That is true," said Hannie.

I was glad to have the other two Musketeers on my side.

"Let'th have a thnowfight!" said Pamela in a baby voice. "I will make a thnowball!" Pamela waved her hands. "I wear mittenth because I am a baby!" she said. She was wearing gloves.

I was so angry, I stamped my foot. I liked my mittens. Nannie, my stepgrandmother, had knitted them for me.

"It is all your fault," said Jannie. "You could have hurt Pamela. Pamela, are you okay?" She tried to brush snow off Pamela's shoulder.

Pamela frowned at Jannie. "I am okay," she said.

"If you are okay, then why are you so upset?" I asked. I crossed my arms.

"Maybe you should go to the nurse," Jannie said to Pamela. She looked concerned.

I giggled. No one needs to see the nurse because of a measly snowball.

A couple of other people giggled, too.

Pamela looked embarrassed. "Why don't you just be quiet!" she told Jannie.

Jannie stepped back. She looked very hurt. "I was only trying to help," she said.

"I do not need your help," said Pamela. "I am not a baby."

"Fine!" said Jannie. She turned and stomped off the playground.

The bell rang. Pamela gave me a look. Then she turned and stomped off the playground, too.

Now Pamela was angry at me and Jannie. And Jannie was angry at me and Pamela.

# 3

## A New Month, a Different House

All that day, I ignored Pamela and Jannie. I had much more important things to think about. Such as: Today was Friday, the last day of January. It was almost the weekend. I looove weekends. I also love weekdays, because I love school. I love school because I love my teacher, Ms. Colman, and I love seeing all my friends.

But I have gotten off the track.

That night Mommy said to me, "Tomorrow is February first. Are you all packed?"

"Yes," I said.

Now, you are probably wondering why I would have to pack just because it is a new month. Remember, I mentioned the big house and the little house? I live at both of them.

I had better start at the beginning.

A long time ago, when I was little, my mommy and daddy and Andrew and I all lived together in Daddy's big house. Andrew is my little brother. He is four going on five. Then Mommy and Daddy decided to get a divorce. So Mommy moved into her own little house. Andrew and I went with her. Daddy stayed in his big house. We missed seeing Daddy every day.

After awhile Mommy and Daddy each got married again. But not to each other. Mommy married Seth Engle, who is our stepfather. He is gigundoly nice. Seth has his own dog, Midgie, and his own cat, Rocky. So, at the little house, are Mommy, Seth, Andrew, me, Midgie, Rocky, my pet rat Emily Junior, and Bob, who is Andrew's hermit crab.

At the big house are a lot of people. Daddy married Elizabeth Thomas. So she is our stepmother. She is really nice. She has four children of her own. They are Sam and Charlie, who are so old that they are in high school. There is Kristy. She is thirteen and very wonderful. There is David Michael, who is seven like me, but an older seven. He does not go to my school.

That is not all. Daddy and Elizabeth adopted my little sister, Emily Michelle, from a country called Vietnam. Emily is two and a half. I named my pet rat after her. The pets at the big house are Boo-Boo, Daddy's cranky cat, Shannon, David Michael's humongous puppy, Crystal Light the Second, my goldfish, and Goldfishie, Andrew's you-know-what.

There are so many people and kids and pets at the big house that Elizabeth's mother, Nannie, came to help take care of everyone. (She is my stepgrandmother who knitted my mittens.)

Now Andrew and I live at the little house

for a month and at the big house for a month. Emily Junior and Bob move back and forth with us.

Remember when I said I had two of a lot of things? It is true. I have two houses, two mommies, two daddies, two cats, two dogs, two pairs of glasses, two best friends. . . . I even have two stuffed cats, Moosie and Goosie (one for each house), and two pieces of Tickly, my special blanket.

In fact, Andrew and I have two of so many things that I made up nicknames for us. I call us Andrew Two-Two and Karen Two-Two. I got that idea from a book Ms. Colman read to my class called *Jacob Two-Two Meets the Hooded Fang*.

Now you know why I had to pack just because it was a new month. That night I went to sleep at the little house. In the morning Mommy drove Andrew and me to the big house.

"Good-bye!" I said, jumping out of the car. I leaned in to give Mommy an extra-big hug and a kiss. "I will call you tomorrow."

15

"Okay, honey," Mommy said.

Andrew hugged and kissed Mommy too.

Then we ran up the walk to the big house and threw open the door.

"Hi, everyone!" I called. "We are here!"

# 4

# A Surprising Announcement

"All right, class. You may put away your math workbooks," said Ms. Colman on Monday morning.

We had been doing addition problems. They are not as hard as subtraction problems.

I sit in the very first row in Ms. Colman's room. On one side of me is Ricky Torres. On the other side is Natalie Springer. We sit in the front row because we are glasses-wearers. You know what? Ms. Colman is a glasses-wearer too.

I used to sit in the back row with Hannie and Nancy. The Three Musketeers were all together. But I see better from the first row.

"I have an announcement to make," said Ms. Colman.

I sat up straight. I love Ms. Colman's Surprising Announcements.

"Oh, boy!" I said. (I had not raised my hand to say that. I had forgotten. But Ms. Colman didn't get mad. See what I mean about her being gigundoly nice?)

"As you probably know, Valentine's Day is coming soon. It is on Friday, almost two weeks from now," said Ms. Colman.

Well, I almost fell out of my chair. I had completely forgotten about Valentine's Day. And it is one of my favorite holidays. (I love just about any holiday.)

"Oh boy, oh boy, oh boy!" I said.

Ms. Colman raised her hand for silence. I pretended to zip my mouth shut.

"I thought that it would be fun for us to have Secret Valentines this year," Ms. Colman continued. "They are like Secret San-

18

tas. I have eighteen slips of paper here. I will write one person's name on each slip. Then each of you will choose a name from a hat. Whoever you pick is your Secret Valentine."

Ms. Colman looked around the room. "Until Valentine's Day, you may secretly leave notes, goodies, or small gifts in your Secret Valentine's desk or cubby. You may also do favors or good deeds for him or her. The Secret Valentines will be revealed at our holiday party."

Bobby raised his hand. "Can I have my Secret Valentine do my homework for me?"

"No, Bobby," said Ms. Colman. "You know better than that."

"How much should we spend on our Secret Valentine?" asked Pamela.

I turned in my seat and rolled my eyes at Hannie and Nancy. Pamela would ask that, I thought. Pamela and I were still mad at each other. And Jannie and Pamela weren't speaking.

"I will ask you to spend no more than

two dollars on any gift for your Secret Valentine," said Ms. Colman. "The idea is to be thoughtful and fun. You may make cards and gifts during art class. The only rule is that you may not switch the name you draw, unless it is your own name. Now, are there any other questions?"

There were no more questions.

Ms. Colman opened her attendance book. "While I am writing down names," she said, "Omar may water our classroom plants. Audrey may feed Hootie and Evelyn." (Hootie and Evelyn are our class guinea pigs.) "And Karen may change our calendar to February."

I jumped up and ran to the big wall calendar by the door. Changing it is an important job. I took it off its hook, turned the page, and hung it back up. Now it showed a picture of a California condor. That is an endangered bird. Our calendar has a picture of an endangered animal every month.

Omar watered the large fern by the window. He spilled only a little.

Ms. Colman finished writing all our names on the slips, then put the slips in the hat.

I could hardly sit still. It was time to choose our Secret Valentines!

# 5

# My Secret Valentine

It felt as if ten years passed before my turn came. I am a person who has a hard time waiting for things. I watched Addie take a slip of paper. She read the name and smiled. I watched Terri take a slip. She tucked it into her pocket.

I wiggled in my seat. I sat on my hands. I remembered to be quiet.

Then Ricky took a slip out of the hat. He gave a huge smile. "All right!" he said.

At last it was my turn. Ms. Colman held out the hat for me. I reached in. Please let

my Secret Valentine be Hannie or Nancy, I thought. Or maybe Ricky.

I took a slip, then slumped down in my seat to read it. Oh, my land! (That is what my great-aunt Carol Packett says when she is surprised.) Guess who my Secret Valentine was.

## Pamela Harding

Well, I will tell you something. It was a Valentine nightmare.

"Please?" I asked at lunchtime that day.

Nancy took a bite of her peanut-butter sandwich. "No," she said. "I am sorry, Karen, but I do not want to switch with you. I like my Secret Valentine." (She had Addie Sidney.)

I looked at Hannie. I tried to look like a sad puppy. I made my eyes big and I blinked. Sometimes this works with Mommy and Daddy.

"I am sorry, Karen," Hannie said. She

24

opened a Baggie of apple slices. "I do not want your Secret Valentine." (She had Sara Ford.)

Boo and bullfrogs.

No one wanted to switch with me. Even though Ms. Colman had asked us not to switch, I had tried. Ms. Colman probably had not been thinking about me and Pamela when she made that rule.

"No," said Ricky. "Ms. Colman said no switching."

"No," said Natalie. "You are not supposed to ask that, Karen."

I sighed and opened my lunch box. Nannie had made me a chicken-salad sandwich, a thermos of soup, and some cookies. An excellent lunch. I ate it sadly.

"No way!" Omar said. I had just asked him to trade Secret Valentines.

It was recess time. We were out on the playground. I kicked at some snow with my foot.

I had asked seven people. No one would

switch with me. I was stuck with yucky old Pamela.

Double boo. Double bullfrogs.

"Do you want to play hopscotch?" asked Hannie.

"I guess so," I said.

Nancy and Hannie and I did one potato, two potato to see who would go first. Hannie was first. Then Nancy. Then me.

While Hannie hopped, I looked for my Secret Valentine on the playground. She was playing four-square with Leslie, Ricky, and Chris Lamar. She hit Chris out.

"Better luck next time," said Pamela. She likes hitting people out.

"What are you going to do for your Secret Valentines?" I asked Hannie and Nancy.

"I am going to make a nice card in art class," said Hannie.

"I will leave a chocolate Kiss in her cubby," Nancy said as she hopped. "Oops."

It was my turn now. To cheer myself up, I thought about the other Valentines I would send. I would make special ones for Hannie and Nancy. Then I would give littler ones to everyone else in class. Plus I needed Valentines for everyone in both my families. Whew! I would have to get busy soon. I would need more red and pink construction paper. And maybe some more tape and glue and glitter.

"Karen, you missed," Hannie called.

I looked down. My foot was on a line. "Oops," I said. "Your turn, Hannie." I smiled. I felt much better now.

# 6

# Let's Put on a Show!

After school that day Nannie fixed Andrew and David Michael and me a snack. We had cheese and crackers and hot chocolate.

"Thank you, Nannie," I said when I had finished. "I am going outside to play."

"Um . . . are you going to play with Hannie?" asked David Michael.

"Yes," I said. "Why?"

"No reason," said my stepbrother. "I will come with you. I am going outside anyway."

"Me too," said Andrew.

It had started to snow again. Big, fat flakes stuck to everything. Outside, new snow covered the bushes and cars and sidewalks. It looked pretty.

Andrew and I leaned back and caught flakes on our tongues.

"Do not eat too much snow," Hannie said. "You might spoil your dinner." She and her brother, Linny, were walking toward my house. Linny is nine going on ten.

I laughed.

"Hi, Hannie. Hi, Linny," said David Michael.

Melody Korman and her brother, Bill, came out of their house across the street. Bill had a snow shovel over one shoulder.

"Hi," Melody said. She is seven. She doesn't go to my school. "I think the snow is letting up. Do you guys want to take our sleds to the playground?"

"No. Let's have a snowfight," said David Michael.

"Count me out," said Bill. He is nine. "I

am going to shovel our front walk. My mom said she would pay me two dollars."

"It has not even stopped snowing yet," I said.

Bill looked at the sky and frowned. "I need to earn extra money."

"What for?" asked Hannie.

"I want to buy a new hockey helmet," Bill said. "I was hoping to get one for Christmas, but I didn't."

"I need extra money too," I said. "I need to buy special supplies to make Valentines. I have to make about a million."

"Make a million what? Dollars?" asked Maria Kilbourne. She had joined us just in time to hear me say that.

"No, Valentines," I said. "I have to send tons of Valentines this year." I felt very important.

"I want to give my mom a fancy box of chocolates this year," said Maria. "I was saving my allowance. But then I spent it on souvenirs at the Ice Capades."

"You saw the Ice Capades?" said Hannie.

30

"I love the Ice Capades," I said. "I saw it last year, when it was Cinderella. It was so, so beautiful."

"I want to be in the Ice Capades," said Andrew. "I could be a prince."

"This gives me an idea," said Linny.

"What? What?" I asked, bouncing in my snow boots. I love it when people get ideas. (I love it even more when *I* get ideas.)

"We could put on our own ice-skating show," said Linny. "We all know how to ice skate, right? We could make up a play. Then we could perform it on ice. We could charge admission. We could all earn extra money that way."

"That is a great idea," said Bill.

"An ice show, starring us!" I said. I could already see myself, wearing a Cinderella costume. I would skate gracefully across the ice. . . .

"Where would we have it?" I asked. "At the skating rink?"

"No," said Linny. "That would be too expensive."

"We could spray water on the street with a hose," said David Michael. "Then it would freeze into ice."

"No," said Maria. "You cannot do that. Cars would skid and have wrecks."

"Maria is right," said Hannie. "Could we flood someone's yard?"

"That is a good idea," said David Michael.

"Our yard is big," I said. "I do not know if Daddy would let us flood it, though. I could ask."

"Maybe Sam or Charlie could help us," said David Michael.

"We also need to sell tickets ahead of time," I said. "So we will all have our money before Valentine's Day. And at the show, we can sell refreshments. So we will make even more money." I jumped up and down. I was getting gigundoly excited.

"We need a name for our show," said Maria.

"And we should ask Scott and Timmy Hsu to be in it," said David Michael.

"We could put on Cinderella," I said quickly. "I could be Cinderella."

"Why can't Hannie be Cinderella?" asked David Michael.

I looked at him.

"No. We need a show we can *all* star in," said Maria.

I shrugged. I cannot help it if I like to be the star.

"How about Snow White?" I said. "I can be Snow White. You can all be dwarves. The dwarves are very important."

"Karen!" Hannie laughed. "You cannot be beautiful Snow White and make us the dwarves!"

I laughed too. "I guess not. Sorry."

"Hannie is right," said David Michael.

I looked at him again.

"Listen, everyone," said Linny. "If we are going to do this, we need to work fast. We need to make tickets and sell them. We need a name and a script for our show. We need to get the rink ready."

"We need costumes," said Maria.

"We need to advertise," said David Michael.

"We need to make food," said Andrew.

We agreed to meet two days later. Our homework was to think up names for our show. Then we would vote.

Linny was taking charge, but I did not mind too much. Our ice show was going to be amazing, no matter whose idea it was.

# 7

## David Michael's Surprising Announcement

At home I took off my snowsuit, snow boots, hat, and mittens. Then I dried my glasses and ran upstairs.

Hannie and I had volunteered to make tickets. We were each supposed to make twenty (although we would probably need more).

I did not have any red or pink construction paper left, but I had plenty of other colors. I sat down at my desk and cut the paper into fat strips.

David Michael tapped on my door. "Are you busy?"

"Yes," I said. "I am very busy."

"So who are you going to make Valentines for?" he asked. He came into my room and sat on my bed.

"Oh, everyone," I said. I cut the paper strips into smaller pieces. "Tons of people."

"What about Hannie?" David Michael asked.

"What *about* Hannie?" I asked. I turned to look at him. "First you wanted her to be Cinderella. Then you said she was right about not being a dwarf. Why are you so interested in Hannie today?"

"No reason." David Michael frowned. "I was just wondering if you were going to send her a Valentine."

"Of course I am going to send her a Valentine," I said. "She is one of my best friends!"

David Michael was quiet.

When I had a nice pile of strips, I began to make a swirly design around their edges.

"I wonder if . . ." David Michael mumbled.

"What?" I said. I counted my strips. I had twelve. That was a good start.

"I wonder if I should send Hannie a Valentine." David Michael spoke so softly, I could hardly hear him. But I did.

I put down my marker. "David Michael," I practically shrieked. "Do you like *Hannie*?"

"No!" David Michael crossed his arms over his chest. "Of course not. I just, you know . . . think she is nice."

Well, let me tell you. I almost had a heart attack. My own stepbrother was in love with my best friend!

"Oh. My. Land," I said.

David Michael was blushing. He looked embarrassed. He looked miserable. That is what love can do to you, I thought. I decided to be kind to him.

I pretended it was no big deal.

"Hmm," I said, tapping my pencil against

my chair. "I think it would be very nice if you sent Hannie a Valentine." Inside I was practically bursting with excitement. "I am sure she would be happy to get it."

"You think so?" asked David Michael. He looked less miserable.

"Oh, yes," I said. I turned around in my chair. I pretended to draw more tickets.

"Okay," said David Michael. "I will." He bounced off my bed and left my room.

After he was gone, I sat and thought for a moment. Valentine's Day was a very special holiday. It was all about love. Kind of like Christmas. I was going to send lovely Valentines to everyone I cared about.

But then there was Pamela. My Secret Valentine. I was stuck with her. I might as well be a good Secret Valentine. If Pamela had picked *my* name, I would want *her* to be a good Secret Valentine.

So what could I do for her?

I could make a nice card.

I could do a good deed.

Finally I decided to hide a small gift in her cubby. Downstairs in the kitchen, I took out a box of fancy cookies. I put some in a Baggie and tied a pink ribbon on it. Then I wrote "From your Secret Valentine" in my best handwriting.

I thought anyone would be glad to get cookies from a Secret Valentine. I felt happy.

# 8

# Pamela's Good and Bad Surprises House

"I know a seeeeecret," I sang to Hannie the next morning.

We were sharing a seat on our school bus. When I am at the big house, I ride to school with Hannie. When I am at the little house, I ride to school with Nancy.

"What secret?" Hannie pushed off her earmuffs.

I smiled. There is nothing better than knowing a secret that is sort of okay to tell.

"Well," I said, "it is about you . . . and a certain *boy*."

"A boy?" Hannie frowned.

"Yup," I said. "A certain boy who likes you." I waited for her to bounce in her seat. I waited for her to beg me to tell her who. I waited for her to say *please, please, please.*

"Ew," said Hannie. "Ick."

*"Hannie,"* I said. "I know a boy who likes you. Don't you want to know who?"

Hannie wrinkled her nose. "Not really. It is just a *boy.*"

"But Hannie. It is David Michael. David Michael, my very own stepbrother, wants you to be his Valentine."

"Yuck," said Hannie. "I do not want to be anyone's Valentine. Except yours and Nancy's and my parents'. Boys are icky. They are gross. This morning Linny spit milk through his *nose.*"

"Ew," I said. "But David Michael is not gross. Well, not *too* gross."

"He is a boy," said Hannie.

I sighed. I felt bad for David Michael. He wanted Hannie to be his Valentine. But she did not want to be. At least, not *yet.* Maybe

Hannie would change her mind by Valentine's Day. Maybe by then she would not think boys are too gross.

I had a brilliant idea.

I would send David Michael Secret Valentine cards and gifts. Then, at the last minute on Valentine's Day, I would tell Hannie what I had done, and she could step in and pretend *she* had sent them to David Michael. My brother would be so happy..

*Yes,* I thought. It was an excellent plan. I just looove Valentine's Day!

When we got to school, I ran inside. No one was in our classroom. So no one saw me hide the Baggie of cookies in Pamela's cubby.

"Hank, would you please take attendance for me?" asked Ms. Colman.

Boo and bullfrogs, I thought. Taking attendance was an important job. I wanted to do it again.

"Oh!" said Ricky, next to me. He held up

a card with a picture of a dog on it. It said, "Doggone it! Will you be my Valentine?" It was signed, "Your Secret Valentine."

I had not gotten anything from my Secret Valentine yet. But then, not everyone would get a card or gift every day.

Pamela smiled and held up her Baggie of cookies. "Look what I found in my cubby!" she said. "I have a good Secret Valentine."

I smiled to myself. Even though Pamela had called me a dumbhead (I had not forgotten that), it was fun to see her happy about her Secret Valentine.

"What is this?" said Pamela, holding up a folded note.

"What does it say?" asked Leslie.

"It says, 'Violets are blue, roses are pink,' " Pamela read. " 'You do not know it, but your feet sure do stink. From your Secret Valentine.' "

I raised my eyebrows. I had not sent that note.

"That is mean," said Leslie.

"Yes, it is," said Pamela. "Why would my

Secret Valentine send me nice cookies and a mean note?"

"Maybe he has a split personality," Bobby suggested.

"All right, class," Ms. Colman said. "I know you want to talk about your Secret Valentines, but it is time for science."

I took out my science book. I did not know who had left that mean note for Pamela. A lot of kids do not like her very much.

It was a mystery.

# 9

# Karen's Great Idea

"*Valentine List*," I wrote at the top of the page. I was at my desk before dinner on Tuesday evening.

I had to be organized. I had a lot of Valentines to make. I could not buy the supplies until we sold tickets to our show. But I could make a list.

BIG HOUSE

Daddy, Elizabeth, Andrew, Kristy, David Michael, Nannie, Emily Michelle, Sam, Charlie

LITTLE HOUSE

Mommy, Seth

I would not send Valentines to any of the animals.

SCHOOL

Ms. Colman, Nancy, Hannie, Ricky, Addie, Audrey, Tammy and Terri, Sara, Bobby, Hank, Ian, Omar, Chris, Natalie

Then I added Leslie, Jannie, and Pamela. I guessed I could not leave out those three. But their Valentines would be very small. Did I need to send Pamela one from me *and* one from her Secret Valentine? I could not decide.

I had to get started on my plan for David Michael's Secret Valentine. Since I did not have red or pink construction paper, I took a sheet of blue paper and cut out a heart shape. Then I glued it to a piece of black paper folded in half. At the top I wrote "Be

Mine" in glue and sprinkled glitter on it. I used my silver-ink marker for the inside. I wrote, "My heart is black and blue without you. Your Secret Valentine."

I would slip it under David Michael's door before dinner. Oops — I remembered that the Valentine was supposed to be from *Hannie*. She could not slip it under David Michael's bedroom door. So I would put the envelope in our mailbox tomorrow. Then Elizabeth would give it to David Michael as if it had been mailed to him.

I am really, really sneaky sometimes.

I was just getting started on another Secret Valentine for Pamela when Kristy tapped on my door. "Karen, dinner!"

"Coming," I called. I hid David Michael's card in my desk and ran downstairs.

There are so many of us at the big house that we eat dinner at a very long table with two benches. I squeezed onto a bench next to my favorite big sister.

"Were you doing homework?" Kristy

asked. She passed me a basket of bread.

"No," I said.

"Tomorrow is the first official meeting for our ice show," said David Michael.

Nannie put some lasagna on my plate. Yum! There was a very delicious salad also.

"What ice show?" asked Daddy.

David Michael and Andrew and I told him about our plans for the show.

"I am already making tickets," I said. "But we need a name."

"How about Ice Capades Junior?" said Andrew.

"No." David Michael shook his head.

"Let's see," said Kristy. "We can all try to think of a name for you."

I beamed. Kristy is so helpful.

"How about the Cutting Edges?" Nannie suggested.

"I like that," said David Michael.

"What about the Skating Sensations?" said Daddy.

"How about Fire on Ice?" said Charlie.

"You could all skate around with sparklers in your teeth."

"Charlie," said Elizabeth. She gave him a Look.

"Ooh," I said. "I know. The Icebreakers." The Icebreakers sounded very cool.

"I like it," said David Michael.

"Me too," said Andrew.

"We can vote on it tomorrow," I said. "But I really hope everyone likes it."

"Now we just need a story for our show," said David Michael.

"Well, I thought of the name," I said. "Someone else can think of the story."

# 10

# The Icebreakers

On Wednesday afternoon all the neighborhood kids met in front of Daddy's house.

"Daddy said we can use our backyard," I reported. "And Sam told me how to make an ice rink. It is easy, but I will need help."

"We can all help after this meeting," said Linny.

"I say we should have the show on the Sunday after Valentine's Day," said Scott Hsu. "That way we will have plenty of time to get ready."

"We have a lot to do," said Linny. "Let's make a list of who will do what."

"Hannie and I will sell the tickets," I said.

Linny wrote that down. "I think we should make our own costumes," he said.

We all agreed.

"Timmy and I will sell the refreshments," said Scott. "We will make hot chocolate, popcorn balls, and bags of peanuts."

"Yum!" I said.

"I will choose music for the show," said Melody.

That's when David Michael and Andrew and I told everyone about an idea I had had.

"The Icebreakers are like policemen on ice," said David Michael. (He had thought up a cops-and-robbers story.)

Linny frowned. "I was thinking about being space rangers."

"I wanted to put on a fairy-tale," said Melody.

"I like the Icebreakers," said Timmy.

"I like it too," added Maria.

We voted. I crossed my fingers on both hands and tried to cross my toes inside my snow boots. The Icebreakers won.

David Michael would write a script. Linny and Maria were going to work on some skating routines.

Hannie and I had to finish making our tickets and then sell them. It was practically the most important job of the whole show.

But first we had to make our ice rink.

In Daddy's backyard, we marked off a very large rectangle. Then we built snow walls about six inches high all around the rectangle. Then we all stomped around inside the rectangle. We packed the snow down very hard and flat.

Later in our rink I would run the hose for several hours. The water would freeze into ice. I would add more water every night until the show. Then we would have a great ice rink!

# 11

# Another Secret Valentine Plan

Hannie and I ran inside the big house to finish our tickets. (Hannie had brought hers over.)

We settled down at the kitchen table. Nannie was starting to make dinner.

"How much should we charge for each ticket?" Hannie asked.

Nannie helped us figure out the math. We decided three dollars was fair.

"Whoa!" said David Michael, coming into the kitchen. "It's cold out there." He smiled at Hannie. She kept writing "The Icebreakers" on her tickets.

"Oh, here, David Michael," Nannie said. She handed him an envelope. "This was in the mail today for you."

It was the Secret Valentine card I had made for him! I pretended to pay no attention.

David Michael ran upstairs with it. Hannie did not even look up. I sighed to myself. This Secret Valentine plan had better work.

The next day at school I found a heart-shaped cherry lollipop hidden in my desk. I had put a card in Pamela's coat pocket when she was at the water fountain. Yesterday she had gotten *another* mean note and a wilted flower. But not from me.

Having Secret Valentines was so, so fun. Omar's Secret Valentine had gone overboard. He got something every day, and sometimes twice a day. So far everyone had received at least one thing from his or her

Secret Valentine. Everyone, that is, except Nancy.

"What is wrong with her Secret Valentine?" I whispered to Hannie at lunch on Thursday. Hannie had gotten a heart-shaped eraser one day, and some caramels another day.

"I do not know," said Hannie. We watched Nancy in the lunch line, buying her milk. Hannie took a bite of macaroni and cheese. "I wonder who her Secret Valentine is. He is being very lazy."

"Or she," I said. "Maybe it is Pamela."

"Maybe. I feel bad that Nancy is not getting any Valentine surprises," said Hannie.

"We have to do something," I said. "We have to be her Secret Valentines."

"That is a great idea," Hannie said with a smile. "We will take turns."

"I will go first," I said. "I have a brand-new pencil with a swirly pattern on it. Nancy has not even seen it. I will sneak it into her desk during recess."

"Good. I will bring something tomorrow," said Hannie.

"What will you bring tomorrow?" Nancy asked as she sat down next to us.

"Oh, nothing," Hannie said. When Nancy was not looking, Hannie smiled at me.

I smiled back. I was so full of Valentine secrets, I felt as if I would burst.

# Get Your Tickets Right Here

"Would you like to buy a ticket to the amazing Icebreakers show?"

Hannie and I smiled at Daddy and Elizabeth and showed them one of our tickets. It was Saturday, eight days before our show. Hannie and I had finished the tickets. They looked beautiful.

"We would love to buy some tickets," said Elizabeth. She reached for her purse. "Let's see. We need . . . seven."

"You do not have to buy one for Emily

Michelle," Hannie said. "Children under three are free."

"Okay," said Elizabeth. "We need six tickets then."

We gave her the tickets and she gave us eighteen dollars. We wrote down the ticket sale on a piece of paper. So far it looked like this:

Mrs. Papadakis: 2 tickets — $6.00
Mrs. Brewer: 6 tickets — $18.00

(Mrs. Brewer is Elizabeth.)

"Thank you very much," I said. "We have to go sell more tickets now."

"Karen, please remember the rules," Daddy said. "You may only sell tickets to families we know. You may not go off our street. You must do all your selling while it is light outside. And no pouting if someone says no."

"I remember, Daddy," I said. "Come on, Hannie."

We sold tickets to the parents of everyone in the show. We had a lot more tickets to sell, but it was time for lunch. We were eating at the big house.

"After lunch we can ask the rest of the people in the neighborhood," said Hannie.

"Yes," I agreed. "And I will call Mommy and Seth."

"You are doing a very good job of selling tickets," said David Michael. He smiled at Hannie. She took a sip of milk. She did not know it yet, but she had already sent him two cards and a small box of redhots.

"I cannot wait to see your show," said Kristy.

"It is going to be wonderful," I said. "Will you be able to help me with my costume?"

Kristy smiled. "Of course."

By Sunday afternoon Hannie and I were a little tired of ringing doorbells and counting money and writing things down. But guess what. We had sold almost every ticket!

"Keep the rest of the tickets," said Linny. "We can sell them at the show, in case anyone who's walking by wants to see it."

David Michael read us the script for our show. It was about a boy who is poor. He robs a bank. A rich girl meets him and feels sorry for him. She helps the poor boy get a job. Then an evil girl tries to ruin the two friends. Then two good police officers save them. The end.

We all liked it a lot. I wanted to be the rich girl. But we wrote our names on slips of paper and picked them out of Scott Hsu's pom-pom hat.

This was our cast list:

Director: David Michael Thomas
Rich Girl: Maria Kilbourne (Boo and bull-frogs.)
Poor Boy: Bill Korman

Evil Girl: Karen Brewer (I cheered up. It would be fun to be evil.)
Girl Police Officer: Hannie Papadakis
Boy Police Officer: Scott Hsu
Butler: Andrew Brewer
Narrator: Linny Papadakis
Music: Melody Korman
Refreshments: Timmy Hsu

Now I was gigundoly excited. The role of the Evil Girl was important. I could make it very dramatic.

After we decided on the cast, we split up the money we had collected. Then we each gave Scott and Timmy three dollars to buy refreshments and plastic cups and paper napkins. After that we each had eight dollars and twenty-five cents left over.

Now I could go buy Valentine card supplies, and a small present for Pamela, and a small present for David Michael from Hannie. Not only that, but I was going to be Evil Girl. Yea!

# 13

# Secret Valentine Gifts

On Monday I found two chocolate Kisses and a note in my cubby. The note said "Sweets to the sweet."

Nancy still had not gotten a single thing from her own Secret Valentine. So Hannie put a card in Nancy's desk. It said, "Valentines once, Valentines twice, As my Valentine, You're so nice." Hannie had written it herself.

I decided to give Nancy my chocolate Kisses after lunch.

We also had show-and-share on Monday morning.

I raised my hand high and waved it around. Finally Ms. Colman called on me.

I stood in the front of the room and held one of our Icebreakers tickets above my head.

"My friends and I are putting on an ice-skating show," I said. "Hannie will be a police girl on ice." Hannie smiled in the back of the room. "I will be an evil villain. Our show will be next Sunday at ten o'clock in my backyard. If any of you are in the neighborhood, you may come. Tickets are three dollars. Thank you." I sat down. I turned around to look at Hannie, and she gave me the thumbs-up sign. Nancy wasn't smiling. Uh-oh, I thought. What is wrong with Nancy?

At lunchtime Nancy told me what was wrong.

"You and Hannie have been talking about

the Icebreakers for days now," Nancy said. "It is like you are the Two Musketeers together, and I am the One Musketeer alone."

"You are right," I told Nancy. "But it is only because you live in the little-house neighborhood."

Nancy looked very sad.

"I have an idea," said Hannie. "There is no rule about who may be in the Icebreakers. Maybe Nancy can help too."

"Really?" said Nancy. "What can I do?"

"Um," I said. "The thing is, we have already divided up the money."

"I do not care about money," said Nancy. "I just want to be with you guys. I do not even have to skate in the show."

"Oh," I said. "Well, I am sure Timmy Hsu will need help with the refreshments."

"And you could sell tickets on the day of the show," said Hannie.

Nancy smiled happily. So did Hannie. So did I. When you are the Three Musketeers, you have to stick together.

* * *

I felt excited as I ran up the walk to the big house after school. I had many things to do that afternoon.

"Hello!" I called from the front hall.

"Hello, dear," said Nannie. "Come into the kitchen and have a snack."

David Michael and Andrew were already there. So were Kristy and Emily Michelle.

"Hello, hello, hello, hello," I sang. Nannie had fixed a snack of rice cakes and peanut butter.

"I have to go to the grocery store this afternoon," said Nannie. "You kids may either stay here with Kristy or come with me."

"I will stay here," said David Michael.

Andrew looked at Kristy. "Will you play Candyland and Cootie with me?"

Kristy nodded. "Sure."

"I will stay here too," said Andrew.

"I would like to go," I said, bouncing in my seat. This was perfect! I could buy my Secret Valentine presents.

"Fine," said Nannie. "It will be you and me and Emily Michelle, then."

While Nannie pushed Emily Michelle in the grocery cart, I set off to find good presents.

And I did. In the beauty aisle I found a very lovely hair barrette for Pamela. It had ribbons wrapped around it and little beads on the ribbons. It was very fancy, and Pamela could wear it with almost anything. I hoped she would like it.

For David Michael I went to the toy section. One of his favorite action figures is Galaxy Man. I bought him Galaxy Man's floating power surfboard. I was very pleased with these two presents.

In the stationery aisle I found construction paper, glitter, and glue. In the baking aisle I found lacy paper doilies. Now I had everything I needed for Valentine's Day. Which was good, because I had spent every penny of my ice-show money.

# 14

## Places, Everyone!

On Wednesday afternoon Nancy rode home with Hannie and me on our school bus. It was fun having the Three Musketeers together on the bus.

We went to my house. "Hi, girls," said Nannie.

"Hi, Hannie. Hi, Nancy," said David Michael. He was already eating his snack. He gave Hannie a special smile.

"Hi," said Hannie. She did not smile back at him.

Uh-oh. It looked as if Hannie still did not

like boys very much. I hoped she would change her mind today or tomorrow. She had been sending David Michael Secret Valentine cards and gifts all week. And she did not even know it.

After Nannie gave us a snack, we ran outside. The other members of the Ice-breakers were already there.

Hannie and I explained that Nancy wanted to help. Everyone thought that was fine.

We tested the ice in our ice rink. It was smooth and thick. Perfect!

David Michael clapped his hands. "We need to rehearse our show," he said. "Does everyone know their parts?"

"Yes!" we cried.

Linny narrated while we skated around each other and tried to be graceful. We practiced our lines. Bill acted sad when he was poor, and happy when he was rich. You may not believe this, but I was good at acting evil.

By the time Nancy's mother came to pick her up, we could tell the Icebreakers show was going to be a big success. We planned to meet again on Friday for another rehearsal.

# Secret Valentine
# Meanie-Mo

"Today we will make decorations for our Valentine's Day party tomorrow," Ms. Colman said on Thursday.

"Yea!" I cried.

"The party will be at lunchtime," she continued. "Instead of going to the lunchroom, we will eat in our classroom. Then we will have special Valentine's Day refreshments. And we will find out who our Secret Valentines are."

I wiggled in my seat. I could not wait to find out who my Secret Valentine was.

This morning I had found a heart-shaped sugar cookie in my desk.

What would Pamela think when she found out I had been her Secret Valentine? I had been a good Secret Valentine. But would she blame me for the mean things she had gotten? Someone was still sending Pamela mean notes almost every day. And once this week she had found a dried-up bug on her desk. It had been very gross. But it had not been put there by me.

Every night that week I had made valentines. I would finish the last ones that night. The ones I had made for Nancy and Hannie were very beautiful and very special.

I still had not told Hannie that I had been pretending she was David Michael's Secret Valentine. By now I was sure that she could not *still* think he was icky. She would be so glad that I had helped her. And wait until she found out that she had bought David Michael a Galaxy Man floating power surfboard!

I decided to tell her that afternoon on the bus ride home from school.

"You did what?" said Hannie, her eyes wide.

"I took care of everything for you," I repeated. We were sharing our usual bus seat.

"I cannot believe you did that," Hannie said. "Did you tell him they were from me?"

"Not exactly," I said with a smile. "I just signed them 'From your Secret Valentine.' But tomorrow you will say they were all from you."

"No, I will not!" said Hannie. She looked angry. "I told you I did not want to be David Michael's Valentine. How could you do this to me?"

"How can *you* be so mean to David Michael?" I asked. I was starting to feel angry too. "It is selfish of you not to be his Valentine. And after all the work I did for you."

"I did not ask you to do it. In fact, I wish you had not." Hannie crossed her arms over her chest. She frowned and looked out the window.

"What will happen tomorrow?" I asked. "David Michael will want to know who his Secret Valentine is."

"That is not my problem," said Hannie.

"I spent some of my ice-show money on David Michael's Galaxy Man floating power surfboard," I said.

Hannie just looked at me.

"You need a Valentine!" I cried.

"No, I do not," said Hannie. "I have Nancy and my parents. I thought *you* would be my Valentine too. But now I am not sure."

My mouth dropped open.

"Guess what," I said angrily. "I made you a Valentine, but now I will throw it away!"

"Good," said Hannie. Her lower lip stuck out.

"Fine," I said. I was so mad I was about to cry. Old meanie-mo Hannie.

Then I had a bad thought: Hannie and I still had to be in the Icebreakers together.

Boo and bullfrogs. Bull and boofrogs.

I thought about David Michael, waiting to find out who his Secret Valentine was. It would be nobody.

## 16

# Red and White

On Friday morning when I woke up, my first thought was: I am sooo happy, because it is Valentine's Day. We would have the class party and find out who our Secret Valentines were. I would hand out all my special Valentines.

Then I remembered my fight with Hannie. She and I would not celebrate together. She would not give me a Valentine. I would not give her one. (I had said that I would throw hers away. But I had not.) And I would have to tell David Michael that *I* was his Secret Valentine.

Ugh. I decided to wait until after school.

Even though I was sad, I still dressed up. I wore a red turtleneck, a red-and-white plaid kilt, a white sweater vest, and white tights with little hearts on them that Mommy had given me. I put a red ribbon in my hair. I looked very Valentinesy.

Downstairs, the people in my big-house family were hugging and kissing and wishing each other Happy Valentine's Day.

At each of our places were Valentines from everyone else in our family.

Plus, Daddy and Elizabeth gave each other presents. Elizabeth gave Daddy a red tie with white hearts on it. Daddy gave Elizabeth a heart-shaped charm for her bracelet.

I felt a little better because everyone around me was so happy.

Nannie had made a special all-red breakfast: bacon, heart-shaped waffles colored

red with food coloring, and strawberries. Yum!

"I wish every day was Valentine's Day," said Andrew, taking a bite of waffle.

"Me too," said David Michael. He seemed extra happy this morning. I thought I knew the reason why: He was expecting to find out who his Secret Valentine was today. Suddenly I lost my appetite. I could not finish even one waffle.

# 17

# Secret Valentines
# Revealed

I could not think about schoolwork that morning. I wanted our party to begin.

I had not talked to Hannie all morning. We each talked to Nancy, and Nancy talked to both of us, but Hannie and I did not even look at each other. I had hoped that Hannie would tell me she had changed her mind, but she did not.

"Class," Ms. Colman finally said, "it is time for our party. You may take out your lunches and eat wherever you wish. When you are done with your lunches, we will have punch and dessert. Then we will play games and reveal the identities of our Secret Valentines."

I jumped up almost before she was finished speaking. Nancy and Hannie and I ate lunch together in the back of the classroom. We ate quietly, since Hannie and I were not speaking.

"I wish you guys would make up," Nancy complained. "This will not be a very fun party if two of the Musketeers are not speaking."

Hannie and I did not say anything. Nancy sighed.

Things got better when we had our punch and dessert. One of our room parents had made heart-shaped cookies. Another one had made delicious cupcakes with pink icing and red sprinkles.

Then we played fun games such as tape-the-heart-on-the-person and musical chairs.

Then Ms. Colman clapped her hands and smiled. "All right, class. Now is the moment you've all been waiting for."

I felt a tingle go down my back.

"Please hand out your Valentines now. Remember to sign the one for your Secret Valentine," Ms. Colman said.

I ran to my desk and pulled out a stack of Valentines. I had made a small Valentine for every single person in my class. I had made extra-nice ones for Ms. Colman, Ricky, and, of course, Hannie and Nancy. (But I had not brought Hannie's.) I had also made a very nice card for my Secret Valentine, Pamela. When she was across the room, I put it on her desk, along with the barrette. I had wrapped it in red-and-white paper.

I kept looking over at my desk. A growing pile of Valentines was on it. One of them was from my Secret Valentine. I could not wait to find out who it was. And who was Nancy's? Why had he or she done such a bad job?

Soon Ms. Colman called, "Is everyone done?"

"Yes!" we all cried.

"Then you may sit down and open your Valentines," she said.

I raced to my desk and sat down. The first thing I did was count all my Valentines. I had sixteen! I found one from Nancy and opened it. She had made it herself. It was very beautiful. My name was written on it in pink sparkly glitter. I love glitter. It makes things look fancy.

I got Valentines from everyone in my class (except Hannie). Then, at the very bottom of my pile, I found my Secret Valentine's gift. I opened it.

"Yes!" I cried. It was a pair of white tights with green shamrocks on them for St. Patrick's Day. They were beautiful. My Secret Valentine must know me very well, to know just what I would like. I turned the card over. It said, "Happy Valentine's Day from your Secret Valentine. Pamela Harding."

Well, for heaven's sake. We had been each

other's Secret Valentines! I could not believe it. She had been a very good Secret Valentine.

"Ms. Colman," said Omar Harris. "Something strange happened. I have two Secret Valentines."

"Really?" said Ms. Colman. She came to his desk and looked at his two cards. Then she looked around the class. "Who was Omar's Secret Valentine?"

Leslie Morris raised her hand. "I was."

"No, I was," said Terri Barkan. "I had Omar's name."

"Oh, my goodness," said Ms. Colman. "There has been a mix-up. Are there any other Valentine problems?"

In the back of the room, Nancy raised her hand. "I have gotten some things from a Secret Valentine," she said. "But today there is no card saying who it was."

I put my hand over my mouth and looked at Hannie. She looked back at me. Neither one of us had gotten Nancy anything for today.

"Who is Nancy's Secret Valentine?" Ms. Colman asked. No one said anything.

"Hmm," said Ms. Colman. "This is very strange. I will start at the beginning."

Ms. Colman went down the roll. Terri had drawn Omar's name. Tammy had drawn her twin, Terri. I had drawn Pamela. (I looked over at her, and she held up her hair barrette and smiled.) I was glad she liked it.

Nancy had drawn Addie Sidney.

Sara had drawn Natalie Springer.

Bobby had drawn Hank Reubens.

Jannie had drawn Audrey Green.

Audrey had drawn Ricky Torres. (Boo and bullfrogs.)

Pamela had drawn me.

Omar had drawn Hannie.

Ian had drawn Tammy Barkan.

Chris had drawn Ian Johnson.

Leslie had drawn Omar too!

Hannie had drawn Sara Ford.

Hank had drawn Jannie Gilbert.

Addie had drawn Leslie Morris.

Natalie had drawn Chris Lamar.

Ricky had drawn Bobby Gianelli.

But no one had drawn Nancy!

"I am very sorry, Nancy," said Ms. Colman. "I must have made a mistake when I wrote out the slips."

"But I did get a few things," said Nancy, looking confused.

"We sent them," I admitted. "Hannie and I. We felt bad that you weren't getting any surprises."

Nancy smiled. "Thanks."

Then Omar offered to give Nancy one of his cards and a gift. Nancy took them happily, even though they said "To Omar" on them. Guess what her gift was? Mitten clips. Nancy would never misplace her mittens again.

"Thank you, Omar," said Ms. Colman. "I apologize again, Nancy."

"I still have a problem," said Pamela, raising her hand. "I have gotten some nice things and some mean things, too. Karen was my Secret Valentine. I think she should apologize for the mean things."

"I did not send anything mean," I said firmly. "I sent only nice things. I promise."

"We will have to get to the bottom of this mystery," said Ms. Colman. "But right now we need to clean up our party things. It is time for our spelling lesson."

Rats, I thought. Our Valentine's Day party was over.

# 18

# The Mystery Solved

During recess that day I showed Nancy my new tights with the shamrocks.

"I cannot wait for St. Patrick's Day," I said.

"You should apologize," Pamela said in back of me.

I turned around. Pamela was wearing her new barrette, but she looked angry. Jannie Gilbert and Leslie Morris were with her. Pamela held up a dog biscuit. "You put this in my desk today."

"No, I did not." I said. Someone else must have put it there."

Pamela stepped so close to me that our noses were almost touching. I glared at her and put my hands on my hips.

"Oh, yeah?" she said.

"Yeah!" I said.

"Um, actually . . ." said Jannie softly.

"Not now, Jannie," snapped Pamela.

"Well, I just wanted to say . . ." mumbled Jannie. "That, um, actually, it was . . ."

Her voice grew softer and softer. I could hardly hear her.

Pamela and I turned to look at Jannie. She seemed embarrassed.

"It was . . . me," she whispered.

"What?" asked Pamela.

"I sent you those things," admitted Jannie. "I was the mean Secret Valentine."

Well, you could have knocked me over with a feather.

Pamela's mouth looked like an O. "Why?" she said.

"I was mad at you for telling me to be quiet after Karen hit you with the snow-ball," admitted Jannie. "I knew Karen was your Secret Valentine, since she asked everyone to trade. I thought she might get into trouble instead of me."

"You sent me the mean poems and the wilted flowers and the yucky bug? And this dog biscuit?" Pamela said. "I cannot believe it."

Jannie looked miserable.

You will never guess what happened next.

Pamela started laughing. I stared at her.

"Jannie, you are a nut," said Pamela.

"You are not mad at me?" said Jannie.

"Well, maybe a little," said Pamela. "But . . . sending all those notes, trying to get Karen in trouble . . ." She started laughing again.

I did not think it was funny. I thought Pamela should be mad at Jannie.

Pamela turned to me. "I am sorry I blamed you, Karen."

"Sure," I said. I crossed my arms and walked away. Behind me I could hear Pamela laughing again. If you ask me, both Pamela and Jannie are nutty.

# 19

## Be My Valentine

Riding home on the school bus that day was not much fun. Hannie and I were still fighting. David Michael was waiting at home for his Secret Valentine, who would never come. I did not feel like rehearsing for the Icebreakers that afternoon because of Hannie. But the show was on Sunday.

I sighed and leaned my head against the bus window. I thought about asking Hannie one last time if she would be David Michael's Secret Valentine. But I did not. I knew what her answer would be. Plus, she would just get mad all over again.

When the bus dropped us off, we went to our own houses without saying good-bye.

Upstairs in my room I pulled out David Michael's card and gift. I had signed the card from Hannie. I could not give it to David Michael now. What about the gift? Perhaps it would help cheer him up when he found out about his Secret Valentine.

I decided to give him the gift and admit that I had sent all those cards. Now both David Michael *and* Hannie would be mad at me. Great. I sighed. How do I get myself into these things?

I picked up his gift and headed downstairs.

"The mail's here!" called Kristy as she came in the front door.

David Michael ran into the front hallway from the kitchen. I stood on the stairs with his gift hidden behind my back.

"Let me see, let me see," cried David Michael.

"Okay, mail hog," said Kristy with a laugh.

David Michael pawed through the mail. I knew there would be no card from Hannie. I got ready to give him his gift.

"Yes!" said David Michael, pulling out a pink envelope.

I was surprised.

He ripped open the envelope and read the card. He smiled.

"What is it?" I asked.

"A card from my Secret Valentine," he said smugly.

"Wha . . . ? Who is it?"

"Margo Pike," he said.

Margo goes to David Michael's school.

"Margo Pike? But I thought you liked Hannie," I said.

"Oh, that was before," he said. "Now I like Margo. And I guess *she* likes *me*."

This had been the most confusing Valentine's Day ever. Nancy had not had a Secret Valentine. Omar had had two. Hannie and I had gotten into a fight. Pamela and I had

been each other's Secret Valentines, but we still did not like each other. Jannie had been the Secret meanie-mo Valentine. David Michael had liked Hannie, but now he liked Margo. I had bought David Michael a gift that he did not need.

I felt as if I needed to sit down.

Slowly I backed upstairs, still hiding the Galaxy Man floating power surfboard. I could save the gift for David Michael's birthday.

Then I had a wonderful thought: There was no need for Hannie and me to be mad at each other anymore!

"I am very sorry I tried to make you David Michael's Valentine," I said.

I had run to Hannie's house and explained the whole thing to her. And I had given her the special Valentine I had made for her. You know what? She had saved my Valentine, too.

"I like the gold glitter," I said. "This is a very beautiful card. Thank you."

"Mine is beautiful, too," said Hannie. "I am glad you did not really throw it away."

I knew that we had truly made up.

Now Hannie and I were on our way to our rehearsal.

I skipped along happily in the snow.

# 20

# The Icebreakers

"Three dollars, please," said Nancy. We sat on stools by the driveway gate, selling tickets. It was almost time for the amazing Icebreakers premiere.

I was in my Evil Girl costume. I thought I looked very cool. I wore white ice skates, black leggings, a black sweatshirt, black gloves, and a black cape made from a towel.

Several people walking by had seen our large Icebreakers sign. That meant we would have a bigger audience. I love performing in front of a crowd.

"Attention, everyone!" said Melody. She blew a whistle. "Please take your seats. The show is about to begin."

I said good-bye to Nancy and hurried to the garage. (All of us performers would wait in the garage.) We had set up lawn chairs and folding chairs in rows outside around the backyard rink. Linny was standing on a box in front.

In the garage, we all wished each other good luck. Hannie and I crossed our fingers. I was so happy we were not mad at each other anymore.

Melody started the music and the audience clapped. I could see everyone in my big-house family, and also Mommy and Seth. It was so gigundoly exciting that I could hardly keep still.

"Once there was a poor boy," Linny began.

Our show had begun.

"Take that, Evil Girl!" cried Hannie, the Girl Police Officer.  ⌐

Hannie pretended to take away my evil powers. She locked them in a box.

"Do not take away my powers!" I cried. "I will be weak!"

"Fine with me," said Hannie. She crossed her arms over her chest. "You belong in jail anyway."

"Oh, no!" I cried. Slowly I skated toward the end of the rink. I crouched down and pretended to be weak. Then, when I was gliding along very, very slowly, I fell over onto my side. (This did not hurt.) "Alas!" I said. "Without my evil powers I am nothing. Oh, no!" Then Hannie and Scott dragged me away and put me in jail. I sat up and shook my fist at them.

"She will not cause any more trouble now," said Hannie. "Ever again!"

The Rich Girl and the ex-Poor Boy celebrated and talked about all the wonderful things they would do now that I was in jail.

Finally Linny said, "The end."

The audience clapped and clapped. We took turns bowing to our fans. Then we

held hands and bowed together. Hannie and I were standing next to each other. Nancy was in the audience, clapping for us.

The Three Musketeers were together again. Yea!

L. GODWIN

## About the Author

ANN M. MARTIN lives in New York City and loves animals, especially cats. She has two cats of her own, Gussie and Woody.

Other books by Ann M. Martin that you might enjoy are *Stage Fright; Me and Katie (the Pest)*; and the books in *The Baby-sitters Club* series.

Ann likes ice cream and *I Love Lucy*. And she has her own little sister, whose name is Jane.

## Little Sister

Don't miss #83

### KAREN'S BUNNY

"Look what the Easter Bunny brought me!" I held up the baby bunny so Granny could see.

"Look!" said Andrew. "His name is Spot."

"Spot is a fine name," Granny said. "And what have you named yours, Karen?"

"Princess Cleopatra," I said grandly. "Princess for short."

"That's a beautiful name," said Granny. "Do you two like your bunnies?"

"Yes, yes, yes!" said Andrew.

"Yes, yes, yes!" I said.

"Oh, my goodness," said Mommy. She and Seth stood in my doorway.

"What's all this?" asked Seth.

"Bunnies!" said Andrew happily.

I looked at Mommy and Seth. They did not look happy. Uh-oh.